The Baddest Kid in Sixth Grade

Not Another Pearson Boy

by J. Walker

This book is dedica**ted** to the daydream**ers** with a plan. We are our only lim**itation**.

Chapter One

You can't tell by looking at me, but I'm pretty cool — not like an athlete or a super genius, I'm middle school cool. Before today the most exciting thing I'd done was camp in my friend Chris' backyard or ride my bike around the neighborhood until the street lights came on. But today things changed.

I've never been class president, but I was voted as treasurer last year. I played sports, too. Football and baseball were my favorites, and whenever a player was hurt the coaches put me in. And when there was a school play I would always be a tree, a rock, or some other *thing* that didn't have lines. That was okay then, but this year I want to be better than okay. I want people to know my name — my real name. When I was class treasurer, nobody in the student government knew my name. They all called me Nate. This year I'm going to make sure that doesn't happen again.

Actually, I wanted to make sure a lot of things don't happen again; like my birthday last year. I invited every single kid in fifth grade to my party. Most of them didn't know me, and my birthday was the perfect time to show them how nice I was so I asked Chris to help me pass out invitations. I spent the whole weekend in my room drawing on, cutting up, and gluing together blue and white construction paper. It took us all day, but Chris and I handed them out to kids in between classes, during recess, and while they hopped on buses after school. We even gave invitations to kids walking home; some of them didn't even go to our school.

When my birth**day** came, I brought all of my board games and ac**tion** figures out to the yard. My br**others** set up every**thing** — ball**oons**, ch**airs**, tables — in the back**yard** while I **help**ed my dad with the food. We **grill**ed enough ham**bur**gers and hot dogs to feed the neighborhood, and my mom made my favor**ite** des**sert**, straw**berry** short**cake**! I was su**per** ex**ci**ted un**til** it got clo**ser** to the time on the in**vi**ta**tions** and hardly any**body** **show**ed up. Only a few of my class**mates** and some of my br**others'** friends came. The worst part was when we got back to school on Mon**day**; the school**yard** was **cover**ed with my blue and white in**vi**ta**tions**.

This year I'm go**ing** to the same middle school as my older br**others**. Dan is in eighth gr**ade** and Rob is in sev**en**th. I **begg**ed my mom to send me to a dif**fer**ent middle school, but she said, "If Wood**son** Middle School is good enough for your br**others** then it's good enough for you." That sucks be**cause** every**where** I go I'm just Dan and Rob's little br**other**. I love them, but I want to be my own man.

Last night my br**others** came in**to** my room to mess with me.

"Hey, Nicky. Are you ready for middle school?" Dan **ask**ed. I ran to the clos**et** and pulled out my out**fit**.

"What do you think?" I **ask**ed hold**ing** up a striped red and white shirt, blue jeans, and my new red base**ball** cap. They **look**ed at each other and **laugh**ed.

"What's so funny?" I asked.

"No, he means are you ready for the teach**ers**?" Rob **ask**ed.

“The teach**ers** are jerks and when they find out that you’re a P**ear**son, they’re go**ing** to be bru**tal**,” Dan said.

“And wait un**til** you meet the prin**ci**pal,” Rob add**ed**. “He nev**er** smiles.” They **laugh**ed some more.

“Why would they be mean to me? They don’t e**ven** know me!”

“They don’t like us and they won’t like you either,” Dan said point**ing** at me.

This could be an**oth**er prank like that time at the zoo. Dan told me that Rob fell in**to** the croc**o**dile pit and that the mother croc**o**dile ate him. I ran as fast as I could to the swamp and saw two crocs as big as cars chew**ing** and fight**ing** over Rob’s orange t-shirt. I **yell**ed and **bang**ed on the glass un**til** a zoo**keep**er came. I **yell**ed, “My br**other**! It ate him!” And I point**ed** to the croc**o**dile that was st**ill** chomp**ing** down on that shirt. I **turn**ed to Dan ho**ping** that he could ex**plain** bet**ter**, but he st**ood** with a blank face and **look**ed at me as if I was speak**ing** French. Then he nod**ded** his head to**ward** a gi**gan**tic rock next to me, and Rob **jump**ed from be**hind** it with no shirt on, smi**ling**. The zoo**keep**er realized what was go**ing** on and **walk**ed a**way** sh**a**king his head. I st**ood** there snotty-nosed with tears roll**ing** down my face. That **happen**ed a few years ago, but I st**ill** think my br**others** are jerks for it. That’s why I don’t believe any**thing** they say. My br**others** are pr**ank**sters.

They might be try**ing** to scare me a**gain**. I said, “I’m not afraid of a few mean teach**ers**.” I lied. I didn’t want them to think I was be**ing** a baby. Now I was feel**ing** nervous about my first day of middle school but be**fore** my br**others** could tell, our mom **walk**ed in.

“Boys, get out of here and let Nicky get some rest. He has a big day to**mor**row,” Mom said. “My boys are growing up so fast.” Dan and Rob left my room with**out** say**ing** an**oth**er word. I **climb**ed in**to** bed. My mom **kiss**ed me on the cheek and said, “You’re go**ing** to have a won**der**ful day, honey. Good**night**.”

◊ ◊ ◊

I woke up to the sound of my mom yell**ing** at the top of her lungs, “Nicky, wake up!” I **open**ed my eyes half**way**, **turn**ed my head and saw 12:00 in flash**ing** red lights. I for**got** to set the alarm! I **jump**ed from the bed and ran to the bath**room** when Mom shout**ed**, “Nicky, there’s no time!” She scoot**ed** me through the hall and down the stairs. I could smell bacon and French toast. *At least break**fast** is ready.* When I got to the kit**chen**, I sat down at the table then my mom **toss**ed a piece of **butter**ed toast on to the pl**ate** in front of me. I held up the burnt bread and **ask**ed, “Where’s break**fast**?”

She said, “I’m sorry, honey, but you were late. Now eat your toast!” I did just that. I was late and wasn’t about to waste more time ex**plain**ing why. Plus, I was st**ill** a little worried about what my br**others** told me last night.

"Mom, what if they don't like me?"

She **turn**ed to**ward** me, **look**ed me straight in the eyes and said, "Oh, honey, of course the other children will like you."

"No not the other kids. I mean the teach**ers**," I said. Mom **walk**ed over and sat next to me.

"Don't worry, honey. Every**one** will like you as long as you . . . ." She raised her hand and then **whisper**ed, "*Shhh.* I think I hear it."

"As long as I what, Mom?"

She st**ood** up and **look**ed out the win**dow**. I **look**ed in time to see the rust**ed** yel**low** school bus turn the corn**er**. Mom ran out of the kit**chen** fast**er** than I'd ev**er** seen her run be**fore**.

"But, Mom, wait!" I said and **follow**ed her in**to** the living room. "You said every**one** will like me as long as I what?"

HONK!!! We **watch**ed through the win**dows** as the bus **stopp**ed in front of our house. "Nicky!" My mom **yell**ed. I tried to give her a kiss good**bye**, but she **grabb**ed me by the shoulders and **push**ed me to**ward** the door. I **turn**ed back but be**fore** I could o**pen** my mouth she said, "Oh Nicky, you should have got**ten** up on time." *HONK!!!* Mom **kiss**ed me on the cheek, spun me around, and then shoved me out the door. Mom was act**ing** strange! *HONK!!!* I faced the bus and saw the dri**ver** point**ing** at me. He **honk**ed the horn a**gain**; this time by ac**ci**dent be**cause** he was bent over the steer**ing** wheel laugh**ing**.

When I got close to the bus, the doors **open**ed. The dri**ver** sat up with a smirk on his face and mumbled, “You P**ear**son.” I couldn’t tell if he was ask**ing** or if he al**ready** knew. “Get in,” he said. I **walk**ed up the stairs to**ward** the big, hairy dri**ver**. Af**ter** two steps the doors closed and the bus pulled off. He drove fast. Ev**ery** bump and turn threw me to the left then to the right. I al**most** fell so I flew in**to** the seat be**hind** the dri**ver**. The engine made a lot of noise but it was qui**et** on the bus. I **look**ed around and saw that I was the only kid on it.

“Ex**cuse** me, sir . . . ?”

“Sir?!” The man said watch**ing** me through the rear-view mir**ror**, “You’re not fool**ing** me, P**ear**son.”

“I . . . I was just won**der**ing, where are the other kids?”

“There are no other kids. This bus is just for you. Now leave me alone!” he shout**ed**.

This was weird, but I didn’t want to say any**thing** else to up**set** him. E**ven** though my house was only a few blocks a**way**, this was the long**est** ride ev**er**. As we drove clo**ser** to the school, the bus **slow**ed down and then **stopp**ed. The doors **open**ed and I st**ood** up. I **walk**ed as fast as I could by the dri**ver** with my head down so that I wouldn’t have to look at him. It **work**ed. I **stepp**ed down and out of the doors.

He **call**ed out from be**hind** me, “Hey, P**ear**son, nice pa**jam**as!” Then he drove a**way** laugh**ing**. I **look**ed down. I was in such a rush this morn**ing** that I for**got** to change clothes. This was not how I want**ed** to st**art** my first day of middle school.

The park**ing** lot was empty. There were no bus**es**. No cars. No**body**. I've been to Wood**son** Middle School a million times and I've nev**er** seen it like this be**fore**. I **walk**ed on the **crack**ed side**walk** look**ing** around at the patchy gr**een** and brown grass. Papers blew in the wind and the garbage cans were **pack**ed with trash. E**ven** the build**ing look**ed old and run**down**. All the red bricks were brown ex**cept** for the ones that were **cover**ed with spray paint. When I got to the front door, I heard some**one** call my name. A lump grew in my throat. The only per**son** who knew my name was that weird bus dri**ver**. I took a deep breath and spun around. It was Chris. He was runn**ing** from across the street. *Whew.* "Chris!" I **call**ed out. We high-fived each other then **walk**ed in**to** the build**ing**.

"You won't believe what **happen**ed to me this morn**ing**."

He **look**ed me up and down then said, "Nev**er** mind that. Why are you wear**ing** your pa**jam**as?" We both **laugh**ed.

E**ven** though the out**side** of the school was run down, the in**side look**ed ex**act**ly the way it did the last time I was here. Orange and black ban**ners hang**ed from the ceiling and the sun **beam**ed through ev**ery** win**dow** onto the lock**ers**. All the class**room** doors were closed and our foot**steps echo**ed all the way down the empty hall**way**.

Chris **follow**ed me into the front off**ice** so that we could ask about our first class. In**side**, an old la**dy** sat at a desk ty**ping** on the com**pu**ter.

"Ex**cuse** me. Can you help us find our class**es**?"

The woman **peek**ed over her screen, smiled and said, “Of course, dear. What are your names?”

“My name is Nick P**ear**son.”

“Did you say P**ear**son?” She **ask**ed and **dropp**ed the smile on her face then sat up high**er** in her ch**air**. I nod**ded** my head. The woman squint**ed** through her thick black glass**es** and **watch**ed me for a couple of seconds. Then she st**ood** up from her ch**air** and ran over to us shout**ing**, “I can’t help you! Get out of here!”

She didn’t seem so old any**more**. Chris and I ran out the door and in**to** the hall.

“Man, what was her prob**lem**?!” Chris **ask**ed. I didn’t know what to say; I was just as con**fused** as he was. We **walk**ed down the hall**way** un**til** we found an o**pen** door. The teach**er** in**side** was stand**ing** at the chalk**board** wri**ting**. Chris **knock**ed and said, “Uhhh, ex**cuse** me. Can you help us find our class?” The man smiled and waved for us to come in.

“I sure can. What gr**ade** are you boys in?”

We both answered, “Six**th**.”

The man **reach**ed in**to** his desk and pulled out a bind**er**. He **flipp**ed through the pages and said, “Six**th**. Got it. Okay, what are your names?” I **elbow**ed Chris.

“I’m Chris Nel**son**.”

“Okay, Chris Nel**son**. You’re in room 103,” he said then **look**ed over at me. “And you, son. What’s your name?”

I smiled ho**ping** that it would sound nice when I said, “Nick P**ear**son.”

The man **slamm**ed shut the bind**er** then got up from his ch**air**. “I want you two out of my class**room**! Now!” He **yell**ed. We barely made it out of the room be**fore** he **slamm**ed the door be**hind** us.

“These people are crazy!” Chris said.

We **walk**ed a few doors down the hall then we heard, “P**ear**son, wait right there.” A man in a dark blue suit **follow**ed us. We **walk**ed a little fast**er** and so did the man in the suit. I had nev**er** seen him be**fore** and **wonder**ed how he knew my name. Chris and I be**gan** to run. The man **yell**ed, “Come back here, P**ear**son,” and **pick**ed up his pace.

“What does he want with you?” Chris **ask**ed.

“Don’t know. Don’t care,” I said try**ing** to run and talk at the same time. Neither of us knew our way around the school so we ran in**to** a dead end. With our backs a**gain**st the wall, we **watch**ed the man in the suit run straight to**ward** us but this time when he **open**ed his mouth to yell, a bell rang.

Chap**ter** Two

The alarm clock rang again. Mom burst through the door — this was just like my dream!

“Nicky, wake up! Your br**others** are go**ing** to leave with**out** you,” she said. Dan and Rob walk to school because it’s only a few blocks away so I’ll have to walk with them and when people see us together they’ll know that we’re br**others**. *That sucks.* I guess it’s too late to ask my mom to drive me to school or to ask Chris’ dad to pick me up.

I showered and then put on my new shirt and jeans and stuck my base**ball** cap into my back pock**et**. When I got to the kit**chen**, every**one** was eat**ing** break**fast**; Mom, Dad, Dan, and Rob were sitt**ing** around the table talk**ing** as if it was a reg**u**lar day, but I was nervous. Six**th** gr**ade** is a big deal. It’s the be**gin**ning of middle school. Next, there’s high school, then college. I'm al**most** a grown up!

“Al**right,** boys, it’s time to go,” Mom announced. My br**others** and I got up from the table and **walk**ed to the front door.

“Be good, boys. We love you,” Dad shout**ed** as Mom **follow**ed us out of the kit**chen**.

◊ ◊ ◊

My first day of six**th** gr**ade** was finally hap**pen**ing! When we got close to school, I bent down and pretend**ed** to tie my shoe**laces** so that Dan and Rob could walk a**head** of me. They didn't e**ven** no**tice** that I **stopp**ed. When I st**ood** up, they were so far a**head** of me that no one would ev**er** think that we were together. I love my br**others** but they're trouble**ma**kers and I *do not* want my new friends to get the wrong i**de**a about me.

Bus**es** and cars lined up in front of the school spitt**ing** out kids then speed**ing** off. The build**ing** **seem**ed big**ger** than I **remember**ed and there were a ton of kids stand**ing** around talk**ing**; some were runn**ing** across the yard hugg**ing** their friends. Groups of kids ran from one side of the build**ing** to the other to hug and high-five other groups of scream**ing** kids. There were some kids hopp**ing** off their bikes and lock**ing** them on street poles. Across the lawn, Dan and Rob **stopp**ed to talk to their friends, but I kept walk**ing** to**ward** the front door and went in**side** the build**ing** to look for Chris. The last time we **talk**ed, he said he'd meet me by the lock**ers**. The prob**lem** was there were so many lock**ers** that I didn't know where to st**art**. There were tons of kids, too. I knew a few of them from fif**th** gr**ade** but there were a lot more faces that I didn't know. I **wander**ed around un**til** I saw Chris. Over the sum**mer** he grew five in**ches**, so he was easy to find. He's al**most** as tall as my dad now and probably the tall**est** kid in our gr**ade**.

"Hey, Chris!" I shout**ed** over other kids talk**ing**, laugh**ing,** and shout**ing** in the hall**way**.

"What's your first class?" he **ask**ed. I un**fold**ed my class schedule.

"I have science with Mr. Gr**een**," I replied. I had heard that name be**fore** but couldn't re**mem**ber where.

"I have art and then English in room 107," he said.

"I have English, too! We're in the same class." *RING!!!* It was time for first period. "I'll see you l**a**ter. Let's meet in front of English class." We high-fived then **walk**ed our sep**a**rate ways.

It took me a few minutes to find the science lab so I was a little late but luckily so was the teach**er**. The room **smell**ed weird but no one else **seem**ed to no**tice**. Kids **walk**ed in be**hind** me and some were al**ready** sitt**ing**. Instead of ch**airs**, there were stools un**der** long black tables: 12 tables and 24 stools. I hurried over to one of the empty tables in the middle of the room and sat down. It's best to sit alone so that people can ch**oose** to sit next to you — my br**other** Dan taught me that. On the table a**gain**st the wall, I saw mi**cro**scopes, shells, and bones. And be**hind** the teach**er**'s desk was a wall of cages. From where I was sitt**ing**, I could see ham**sters** and gerbils runn**ing** on their little wheels or eat**ing**. *That's why the room* ***smell****ed funny!*

The bell rang and every**one** sat down. And the teach**er** finally **walk**ed in. *Mr. Gr**een**!* I knew ex**act**ly who he was. He e**ven** had on the same kind of clothes that he wore when I first met him: a sweat**er**-vest, a white dress shirt, and brown pants. This guy did not believe in change.

I met Mr. Gr**een** last year when my parents were **call**ed to the prin**ci**pal's off**ice**; I **stay**ed home sick that day so I had to go, too. When we got there, Dan and Rob were stand**ing** in the door**way** and a man was sitt**ing** in one of the ch**airs** across from the prin**ci**pal. His back was fa**cing** us. It was Mr. Gr**een**. No**body** said any**thing** so Dad broke the ice.

“Hello, Prin**ci**pal Reese. You want**ed** to see us?” I knew the routine by now. Mom and Dad get a call from the school. They rush over. Prin**ci**pal Reese makes a few threats. Mom and Dad pun**ish** my br**others** and by the next week they're at it a**gain**.

“Yes, Mr. and Mrs. P**ear**son, I'm sorry to say it but I'm sus**pend**ing your boys for the rest of the week. While at lun**ch**, your boys thought it would be funny to throw spaghetti and meat**balls** all over Mr. Gr**een's** car and when he tried to stop them, they threw spaghetti *at* him,” Prin**ci**pal Reese said. Dan giggled and Rob **laugh**ed, too, then Mom and Dad **grabb**ed each of them by their ears and held on for the rest of the meet**ing**. Mr. Gr**een** st**ood** up and faced us and when I saw that spaghetti sauce all over his clothes, I couldn't believe it. I must have made a noise be**cause** he **look**ed right at me. Then he left the room with**out** say**ing** any**thing**.

It took the prin**ci**pal a couple of days to think of a big enough pun**ish**ment for Dan and Rob, but he did. On top of be**ing** sus**pend**ed, they weren't a**llowed** at the dance. This was a big deal be**cause** it was the Hal**lo**ween costume party and all the kids **dress**ed up. The year be**fore**, Dan paint**ed** his en**tire** body gr**een** and spent an hour cutt**ing** up his shirt to look like The Incredible Hulk; He won first-place for best costume.

The next year, when Rob got to Wood**son** Middle School, he want**ed** to win, too, so my br**others** made their costumes. One was go**ing** to be a vam**pire** and the other a vam**pire** slay**er**. Their costumes **look**ed awe**some**! Dan used red dye to make his fangs look bloody, and Rob carved a real tree branch in**to** a wood**en** stake. My mom **even** gave them her make-up so that Dan could look dead and pale. But be**cause** of their sus**pen**sion, they couldn't go to the dance. That was no**thing** com**pared** to Mom and Dad's pun**ish**ment. Ev**er**y week**end** for two months, my br**others** had to wash the car, dust the fur**ni**ture, vac**uum** the car**pet**, sweep the floors, cut the grass, wash their own clothes, scrub the toilet and wash the dish**es** ev**er**y night. Dad e**ven** made them wr**ite** an apology let**ter** to Mr. Gr**een**.

I was an inch or two tall**er** now, but I **look**ed the same and so did Mr. Gr**een**. When he **walk**ed in, he went straight to the chalk**board** next to his desk and scribbled his name. He faced the class and said, "Wel**come** to an**i**mal science. My name is Mr. Gr**een**." He smiled and **look**ed around the room at all the kids but when his eyes land**ed** on me, his face **turn**ed serious. And the wrinkles in his fore**head** be**gan** to show. He said, "Uhhh, class, we are, uhhh, go**ing** to change things up a bit . . . with **assign**ed seat**ing**." Ev**erybod**y **groan**ed and mumbled. No**body** likes **assign**ed seat**ing**. Mr. Gr**een** read our names from the class list in his hand. He start**ed** al**pha**bet**ically** and e**ven** though my last name be**gins** with a *P*, I end**ed** up in the back of the room, alone.

Mr. Gr**een** held up a stack of papers above his head. He said, "This is your per**mission** slip to work with the an**i**mals. It's very im**port**ant that you take it home to have an adult sign it."

He gave the stack to the girl sitt**ing** clo**sest** to him. “Please take one and pass it back,” he said. The girl took hers and **pass**ed the rest back and so did the boy be**hind** her. This went on un**til** the kid in front of me **turn**ed around and shrugged his shoulders. He didn’t have an**oth**er to pass back.

“Mr. Gr**een**, I don’t have one,” I **call**ed out.

“Well, what did you do with it?”

“No**thing** . . . you didn’t pass out enough.”

“Oh, *really*?” he said look**ing** right at me. He **walk**ed to his ch**air** and sat down. “Well, come and get it,” he said. I **walk**ed to the front of the room to his desk. He moved papers around and pretend**ed** not to no**tice** me stand**ing** there. Then he dug un**der** the pile of papers on his desk. When he **look**ed up, he was smil**ing**. “Here it is,” he said and lif**ted** the paper above his desk. I st**ood** with my back to the rest of the class, but I knew ev**ery** eye in the room was on me. Instead of lean**ing** for**ward** to give me the paper, he held it in his left hand and **turn**ed his ch**air** a little so that I had to walk around the side of his desk to grab it. I took a step, then an**other**, and *BOOM! CRASH! HISS! HISS!* I **jump**ed back as fast as I could and al**most** fell. Every**one laugh**ed.

“Calm down, class. That’s just Lucy,” Mr. Gr**een** said. I straightened up, **grabb**ed the paper and **walk**ed really fast to my seat. My heart was st**ill** ra**cing**. “She’s a ferret,” he said, “and she doesn’t like it when people get too close to her cage.” A few kids were st**ill** laugh**ing**. I was glad to be sitt**ing** in the back of the room now. Mr. Gr**een** st**ood** up and **walk**ed over to the board.

E**ven** though he wrote with his back to the class, I could see part of his face. I think I saw him smi**ling** but may**be** not.

“Class, take out a piece of paper and copy this down,” he said. “This is your home**work** for to**night**.” I **reach**ed in**to** my back**pack**, pulled out my yel**low** note**book**, and copied from the board. When I was done, I tore out a sheet of paper in case some**body** **ask**ed me for one, but no**body** did. I felt invisible. No**body** had **look**ed at me since I **walk**ed back from the teach**er**’s desk.

Mr. Gr**een** **talk**ed for a while. I tried to pay at**ten**tion so he wouldn’t think that I was like my br**others**, but he was bor**ing**. He sat at his desk the whole time and sound**ed** as if he was fall**ing** a**sleep**. Or may**be** I was the one fall**ing** a**sleep**. Luckily, it was al**most** time for the next period and I **count**ed down the seconds. I want**ed** to be the first one out of the room and st**art** over in an**oth**er class with new kids and a new teach**er**. The bell rang and be**fore** it **stopp**ed, I was out the door.

Kids ran from class**room** doors and **fill**ed the hall**way**. At first, I didn’t see Chris be**cause** he was sur**round**ed by a group of boys and all of them were al**most** as tall as he was. I could tell that they knew him; most people did. He was kind of like a star in our town, but he nev**er** **seem**ed to care. When I got clo**ser**, Chris said ‘bye’ to his friends and **walk**ed a**way**.

“How was your first class?” he asked.

"It was okay," I lied. I didn't want Chris to think that I was having a bad day. I could tell by the way he smiled that he was having a good morn**ing**, but I **ask**ed any**way**, "How was yours?"

"It was great!" he **yell**ed over the noise from the pass**ing** kids. "The art teach**er** is cool. He **play**ed music while we paint**ed**. And do you re**mem**ber Erica and Kyle from last year? They're in my class."

At least one of us is having a good day. *Oh, crap! My note**book**!* "Hey man, save me a seat. I for**got** some**thing**," I said to Chris. I ran a**way** be**fore** he could answer. I didn't want to be late for my next class but more than that I didn't want to give Mr. Gr**een** an**oth**er reason to not like me. Now I'll have to make up an ex**cuse** for be**ing** back in his class. My heart was beat**ing** so loudly that I **wonder**ed if any**body** else could hear it. I st**ood** at the door long enough to know that there were no kids in**side**. When I **walk**ed in, I ran straight to my table ho**ping** that Mr. Gr**een** wouldn't no**tice** me. My note**book** was gone. I bent down on the floor but it wasn't there.

"Mr. Gr**een**, have you seen . . . ," I said. He wasn't there either. From the back of the room, I saw some**thing** yel**low** on his desk. I **walk**ed fast so that I could get the note**book** and go be**fore** he came back. When I got clo**ser**, I knew for sure that it was my book. I **grabb**ed it and *BOOM! CRASH! HISS! HISS!* Ahhh! This time I fell back in**to** the wall and **dropp**ed my note**book**. I heard a click**ing** sound. I must have **knock**ed some**thing** over, but I didn't stick around long enough to find out what it was. I ran out of there and in**to** English class across the hall.

Chapter Three

I sat down next to Chris in the seat by the door. The bell rang. I made it!

"Hey man, are you okay?"

"Yeah," I lied again. I was sweating and out of breath. Even the teacher noticed. He leaned in and asked, "Young man, are you alright?" I smiled and nodded my head. When he walked away, I took a quick peek around the room just to see if I knew anybody. I saw a girl who was in a couple of plays with me last year, but I didn't really know her.

"Hello class, I'm Mr. Matthews." He told us to look inside of our desks for the reading book and to follow along with him as he read. I tried to pay attention but Chris poked my arm.

"What's up? What happened to you?" Chris asked. I didn't even look at him. I just shook my head and pretended to be reading. He was my best friend but some things were embarrassing. Mr. Matthews saw us and said, "Boys, please follow along." Chris and I apologized. Twenty minutes went by and the teacher was still reading. Everyone followed along, but I couldn't stop thinking about my morning. I wish I could start this day over. Mr. Matthews read with his nose in the pages and didn't notice Chris laugh. I ignored him, but he poked my arm again.

"Nick, look over there," Chris whispered. I kept my eyes on the book. He laughed again and whispered, "*Pssst.* Look in the hallway." This time he pointed out the door and I looked just in time to see a hamster run by our room.

A few seconds l**a**ter an**oth**er one ran by and then three more. Chris **laugh**ed when**ev**er a new an**i**mal ran by the door. I count**ed** five ham**sters**, nine gerbils and then Lucy, the ferret. I sat fro**zen** in my seat. Chris knew me well enough to know that some**thing** was up be**cause** I wasn't laugh**ing**. He **ask**ed, "What's the mat**ter**?" I wiggled and **slouch**ed down in my seat try**ing** to dis**app**ear.

The an**i**mals from science class ran back and forth in front of the door, but no**body** no**ticed** ex**cept** Chris and me. When Mr. Mat**thews** finally **look**ed up from that book it was too late, and Lucy was coming for him. The scream that came from Mr. Mat**thews** was as high as my mom's that time she saw a squirrel in the at**tic**. Mr. Mat**thews** went left and so did Lucy. Then he faked right, but she was on his heels. No mat**ter** where he ran, Lucy **follow**ed and now she was ch**a**sing him around his desk. The ham**sters** and gerbils scrambled un**der** the ch**airs** crawl**ing** be**tween** kids' shoes and jump**ing** on top of back**packs**. Some kids st**ood** on his or her seats and others sat with their legs in the air, laugh**ing**. I **watch**ed Lucy chase Mr. Mat**thews** around his desk so many times that they made me dizzy. It was wild in there! Every**one** was either scream**ing** or laugh**ing** but no one was loud**er** than Mr. Mat**thews**.

"What in the world is go**ing** on?!" Prin**ci**pal Reese shout**ed** from the door**way**. We all fr**oze** once we realized he was watch**ing**. The prin**ci**pal had one hand be**hind** his back and he **scoop**ed up Lucy with the other. She **squirm**ed around for a few seconds but **stopp**ed when he **turn**ed her face to his. I guess she had heard about him, too. A few kids **pick**ed up the ham**sters** and gerbils and put them on the teach**er**'s desk.

"Out**side**! Now!" The prin**ci**pal said to Mr. Mat**thews**.

Prin**ci**pal Reese **follow**ed our teach**er** in**to** the hall**way**. Mr. Mat**thews** **walk**ed slowly with his head down. I felt badly for him. Prin**ci**pal Reese's face was red and his eyes **look**ed as if they were go**ing** to pop out of his head. Prin**ci**pal Reese took a deep breath and start**ed** to speak un**til** he saw ev**er**y eye in the class**room** on him. He **reach**ed for the door and pulled it shut but it didn't close all the way.

"What is go**ing** on in there?! This is a middle school not a pett**ing** zoo!"

"I don't know how this **happen**ed. I . . . ," Mr. Mat**thews** said before the prin**ci**pal cut him off.

"You're runn**ing** around like a mad**man** all be**cause** of this little thing!" Principle Reese said and lif**ted** Lucy eye to eye with Mr. Mat**thews**.

"I'm sorry for the dis**tur**bance. Some of the stu**dents** were frightened and scream**ing**."

"They weren't the only ones who were scream**ing**!" Every**one** knew that Prin**ci**pal Reese **yell**ed at kids, but no one had ev**er** seen him yell at a teach**er**. The prin**ci**pal **look**ed at us in the class**room** then back to Mr. Mat**thews**. He **lean**ed in, **whisper**ed to Mr. Mat**thews,** and hand**ed** him some**thing**. And then he **walk**ed a**way**. Now the room was qui**et** ex**cept** for the ham**sters** and gerbils squeak**ing** on the teach**er**'s desk. I guess they were as scared as we were. Mr. Mat**thews** **push**ed the door o**pen** with one hand be**hind** his back. He st**ood** for a second then **walk**ed to his desk. Prin**ci**pal Reese **rush**ed back in**to** the room with a cage in his hands and put all the animals in**side**. Af**ter** he left, Mr. Mat**thews** st**ood** be**hind** his desk with his head down.

No**body** said a word. It was so qui**et** that I could hear the tick**ing** from the clock above my head. Mr. Mat**thews** lif**ted** up his head, **look**ed around the room then **lower**ed his head again. He raised the hand that was be**hind** his back; in it was my yel**low** note**book**. I couldn't believe it! I al**most** fell out of my ch**air**. *How'd he get it?*

“What's wrong?” Chris **whisper**ed. I shook my head a**gain**.

“Whose note**book** is this?” Mr. Mat**thews** **ask**ed with**out** lift**ing** his head.

Ev**eryone** in the room was qui**et** un**til** Denise Parks said, “Mr. Mat**thews**, what makes you think that note**book** be**longs** to some**one** in *this* class?” Denise went to my el**e**men**tar**y school, and she al**ways** had some**thing** to say about every**thing**. I want**ed** to know why Mr. Mat**thews** **ask**ed our class, too, but I wasn't about to ask him. He **walk**ed around to the front of his desk. The en**tire** time his eyes were on Denise. He said, “This book was found in the science lab next to the cage release but**ton**. To**day** only six**th** gr**ade** has science. The prin**ci**pal has gone to the other six**th** gr**ade** class**rooms** and we are the last one, so I'll ask a**gain**, whose note**book** is this?”

No**thing** but silence. The bell was about to ring but no**body** **pack**ed up. Mr. Mat**thews** **dropp**ed the note**book** on his desk then sat down. He was sweaty and **look**ed as if he'd just run a mar**a**thon. A few more minutes went by of total silence and then finally the bell rang. We all **rush**ed in**to** the hall, but I was the first kid out the door. I **grabb**ed my hat from my back poc**ket** and pulled it as low as I could over my eyes. I want**ed** to hide. Kids st**ood** around talk**ing** so I **push**ed through the crowd to the water foun**tain** and Chris **follow**ed. He **lean**ed a**gain**st the lock**ers** watch**ing** me.

"Nick, what's go**ing** on? When you saw that note**book** you al**most** fell over. Is it yours?" Chris **ask**ed. My brain was ra**cing**. I couldn't say what I want**ed** to say — not here, not now — so I bent over and drank from the foun**tain**. I drank and drank and drank un**til** the hall**way** was empty.

"Was that note**book** yours? Did *you* o**pen** those cages?"

"Yeah, that book was mine. I **open**ed the cages!" I said, "We're go**ing** to be late for class. I'll tell you every**thing** **la**ter, I promise."

"Okay, you bet**ter**!" Chris said. We **slapp**ed hands then he **walk**ed a**way**. When Chris moved I saw Denise Parks stand**ing** a few lock**ers** a**way** with an**oth**er girl. I **wonder**ed if she heard any**thing**. *Nah! She was probably too busy talk**ing** to her friend.*

Chap**ter** Four

I **reach**ed in**to** my pock**et** for my class schedule. Math. And it's all the way on the other side of the build**ing**. When I found the room, I **peek**ed in through the win**dow** at the woman stand**ing** in the front of the class. She was talk**ing** and point**ing** a ru**ler** around the room. I wasn't sure if I should wait un**til** she was **finish**ed talk**ing** or just walk in. It was too late now; she was point**ing** that ru**ler** at the window, right at me. I pulled o**pen** the door.

"Young man, you are late," she **said**. "And take off that cap in my class**room**!" I took off my hat and **stuff**ed it in**to** my back pock**et**.

"I . . . I know. I'm sorry I was on the other side of the . . . ."

"I am not fond of ex**cu**ses," she said with a frown. "What is your name?" she **ask**ed st**ill** point**ing** that ru**ler** at me. I **walk**ed over to her. When I got clo**ser**, I could see all the wrinkles in her face and neck. Her gray hair, black eye**brows,** and dark red lip**stick** made her look like a witch.

"My name is Nick and I'm sorry for . . . ."

She squint**ed** her eyes and said, "Young man, your name? You do have a last name, don't you?" I nod**ded** my head. "Ok, well what is it?" She scared me a little, but I **stepp**ed clo**ser** to her any**way** so that no one else would hear what we were say**ing**.

I nod**ded** my head and said, “P**ear**son.” I **jump**ed back and wait**ed** for her to yell a**gain**, but she didn’t. She cl**eared** her throat then pat**ted** down her hair.

“Nick . . . P**ear**son?” she **ask**ed al**most** in a whis**per** but smiled when she said my name. I nod**ded** my head then **walk**ed to the back of the room to the only empty seat. When I sat down, she **look**ed at me and said, “Wel**come**, I am Mrs. Go**mez**.”

The teacher **pass**ed out cal**culators** then she wrote a few math prob**lems** on the board. I start**ed** to wr**ite** and then felt all the water that I drank fill up inside. I raised my hand but the teach**er**’s back was **turn**ed. I **call**ed out, “Mrs. Go**mez**, may I use the bath**room**?”

“No, you may not. I told you all that there would be no bath**room** breaks dur**ing** my class,” she said with**out** look**ing** a**way** from the board.

“But I came in late and **miss**ed that part.”

She **turn**ed around, **look**ed at me, and said, “I'm sorry dear, of course, *you* can go but hurry back.” I **jump**ed from my seat and **rush**ed to**ward** the door.

“Mr. P**ear**son, you **dropp**ed some**thing**,” Mrs. Go**mez** said and point**ed** to my base**ball** cap that had fall**en** on the floor. I **pick**ed it up, **stuff**ed it back in my poc**ket,** and ran to the bath**room**. Af**ter** I used it, I **lean**ed over to flush the toilet and my base**ball** cap fell in. *Ahhh! My hat!* It spun around and then **disappear**ed.

I **walk**ed back to the class**room** feel**ing** **bumm**ed out. That hat was br**and** new and I had just drawn my initials in it in cool bubble let**ters**. When I **walk**ed in**to** the room, Mrs. Go**mez** was st**ill** writ**ing** on the board. Most of the kids **look**ed up at her and then down at their papers, copy**ing** what she wrote.

But a few kids twist**ed** and **turn**ed and **watch**ed me walk to my desk. *It must be my new shirt!* I **walk**ed by a girl wri**ting** in her note**book** and **remember**ed that I st**ill** need**ed** mine. I wasn't sure how I would get it, but I knew that I wasn't go**ing** to ask for it.

No**thing** crazy **happen**ed in math class. Actually, Mrs. Go**mez** was nice to me, but I'm no dummy — I kept qui**et** any**way**. I thought about how I would ex**plain** to my mom that I lost my base**ball** cap. Af**ter** I copied the notes from the board, I **peek**ed around at the other kids. I could see the whole class and **watch**ed those same kids up front whis**per** to one an**oth**er then look in my di**rec**tion. When I **look**ed at them, they **turn**ed around. At first, I wasn't sure if they were look**ing** at me un**til** it **happen**ed a**gain**. I **wonder**ed what they were say**ing**.

"Al**right** children, please pass for**ward** your cal**culators** and pack up," Mrs. Go**mez** said. It was time for lun**ch**. I want**ed** to run out of that room and in**to** the caf**e**teri**a**. Chris and I met at his locker and **walk**ed together. Kids moved in ev**ery** di**rec**tion. And ev**erybod**y was talk**ing** or push**ing** or m**a**king noise try**ing** to get to the same place. This was so ex**ci**ting! I felt like a foot**ball** play**er** walk**ing** out of the lock**er** room and on**to** the field right be**fore** a game — pass**ing** all his fans — ex**cept** I didn't have any fans and I was only go**ing** to the caf**e**teri**a**.

"I can't wait to meet new people!" I said. Chris made a face. To him, it was no big deal. He didn't un**der**stand be**cause** he was used to people li**king** him and he al**ready** has a ton of friends. He's kind of famous in our town be**cause** he is super smart, makes straight A's, and is a good bas**ket**ball play**er**.

E**ven** be**fore** he grew the five inch**es**, ev**eryone** knew Chris Nel**son**. I was happy to be his friend, but I want**ed** people to know my name, too.

Chap**ter** Five

Lunch**time** is the most im**port**ant time of day. Ev**erybod**y knows that. It's be**cause** where you sit can make you or break you. Middle school is all about the people you know. Dan used to say if no one knows your name then you're do**ing** some**thing** wrong. For a long time I didn't know what that meant, but I think I do now.

I didn't tell Chris that I **plann**ed to make as many friends as I could to**day** and it didn't mat**ter** how. When we **walk**ed through the double doors to the caf**e**ter**i**a, my heart start**ed** to beat fast**er**. This was not like the lunch**room** in my old el**e**men**tar**y school. I saw hardly any adults and a lot of kids weren't **even** eat**ing**, they were just hang**ing** out. Some kids were boun**cing** balls. Some were play**ing** with cards. Some were sitt**ing** on tables fly**ing** paper air**planes**. I st**ood** there t**a**king it all in.

On the left side of the caf**e**ter**i**a, kids lined up at a count**er**. At first, it **seem**ed like a reg**u**lar lun**ch** line un**til** I saw kids walk**ing** a**way** with cookies, chips, and **even** candy. It was a line just for snacks! On the other side of the caf**e**ter**i**a was the reg**u**lar lun**ch** line with trays of pizza, chic**ken** fing**ers**, fruit, and ev**er**y kind of juice you could imagine. The back wall of the caf**e**ter**i**a had a huge win**dow** look**ing** out to the play**ground**. A few kids were out**side** ra**cing** one an**oth**er up and down the field. They were laugh**ing** and having a good time; I want**ed** that to be me. Chris and I **walk**ed to the lun**ch** line and I no**ticed** kids watch**ing** me.

I kept walk**ing** and the eyes **follow**ed. I guess my new red and white shirt was cool**er** than I thought.

Af**ter** gett**ing** in the lun**ch** line with Chris, I heard some**one** say, “Nicky!” Only people in my family call me that. It was Dan. He and Rob were cross**ing** the caf**e**teria to**ward** me, and they were both chee**sing** from ear to ear.

“Is it true?” Dan **ask**ed.

Be**fore** I could ask him what he was talk**ing** about, Rob answered, “Of course, it’s true. He’s one of us.” They high-fived each other and Rob pat**ted** me on the back. Then they **walk**ed a**way**. Chris **ask**ed me what they meant.

“I have no i**de**a,” I said.

Chris and I **grabb**ed our food and made our way across the room to a couple of empty seats. Long tables went from one end of the caf**e**teria to the other. We zig**zagged** around them and moved in and out of the aisles. No mat**ter** where we **walk**ed, we had to dodge people moving around. Out of no**where** some**one** said, “Hey.” I wasn’t sure if he was talk**ing** to me, but I smiled any**way**. We **walk**ed a little far**ther** and then an**oth**er kid said, “What’s up!” May**be** they were friends of my br**others**. The more we **walk**ed the more that people be**gan** to speak to us. Usually people don’t st**art** talk**ing** to me un**til** af**ter** I join a group or act in a play. But to**day** was diff**er**ent. We **walk**ed by a table full of girls and one of them smiled at me. This was the best day ev**er**!

“Hey man, what**ev**er you’re do**ing**, keep do**ing** it,” Chris said.

My cheeks hurt from smi**ling** so much but it felt good to have so many people talk to me. Chris kept ask**ing** me questions, but I was too busy look**ing** around to answer. I want**ed** to see what the other kids were do**ing**. I wasn't sure if go**ing** out for re**cess** was cool un**til** a tall, skinny kid with a foot**ball**, **lean**ed over from his table. He said his name was Mark and he **ask**ed Chris and me if we want**ed** to go out to the play**ground**. We both said yes. It was only the first day of school and things were go**ing** bet**ter** than I **plann**ed.

Out**side** there was a bun**ch** of boys stand**ing** around wait**ing** for some**thing**. We got clo**ser** and I could tell they were wait**ing** for Mark and his foot**ball**. A few of them **call**ed his name and shook his hand all ho**ping** to be cho**sen** for his team. This made me nervous. He did ask us if we want**ed** to go out**side** but he didn't say any**thing** about play**ing** flag foot**ball**. *What if no**bod**y choo**ses** me? Or what if some**one** cool comes out and asks to play?* Mark **look**ed around at the small crowd and **call**ed out, "Mit**chell**, Tur**ner**, Sam**u**els, and P**ear**son." *He **call**ed my name!*

I want**ed** to high-five him, but I **play**ed it cool. Mark **toss**ed the ball to the kid stand**ing** next to him. He said, "Cur**tis**, Br**ooks**, Mill**er**, and you." He point**ed** to Chris. I want**ed** to seem cool so I st**ood** with a serious face and **cross**ed my arms, but I really want**ed** to high-five Chris, too. I don't know why these guys chose us but I didn't care. No one has ev**er** **pick**ed me to be on a team be**fore**. It didn't **even** mat**ter** that Chris and I were go**ing** to play a**gain**st each other. I was just happy to be cho**sen**.

We didn't st**art** play**ing** yet but there was al**ready** a crowd wait**ing** for some**one** to throw the ball and so was I. All ten of us lined up on op**po**site sides of the field then *BURRR!* A whistle blew. It was Prin**ci**pal Reese stomp**ing** across the field to**ward** us. Ev**erybod**y st**ood** st**ill** as if we were play**ing** fr**eeze** tag. He blew the whistle a**gain** and the crowd moved in close to him. Ev**ery** kid in the school was out**side** on the play**ground** huddled around Prin**ci**pal Reese. I couldn't see him be**cause** of the tall**er** kids in front of me, but I heard ev**ery** word.

"If your initials are *NP* step for**ward** now," he said. I **look**ed around at the kids who were m**a**king their way through the crowd.

"Hey," Chris **whisper**ed and then **elbow**ed me in the arm. "N.P." *Oh! I'm an NP.* Now I was one of those kids push**ing** through the crowd while ev**eryone** else **watch**ed. When I got to the middle of the circle, I saw that Prin**ci**pal Reese was hold**ing** my red base**ball** cap. I had no clue how he got it. It fell in the toilet and I **flush**ed it a**way**. All the *NP* kids lined up side by side in front of the prin**ci**pal. He **look**ed down the line at each of us.

"Nadine Platt and Natalie Plum**mer**, you two are dis**missed**," he said. The girls ran out of line and Prin**ci**pal Reese **stepp**ed over to the next kid. "What is your name, young man?"

The boy said his name was Nor**man** Pal**mer**. I didn't know him, but he didn't look like the type of kid to wear a base**ball** cap and Prin**ci**pal Reese knew it.

Most of the boys here wore t-shirts and jeans, but Norman wore a **collar**ed shirt and the kind of pants that I only wear to church.

Prin**ci**pal Reese start**ed** at Nor**man**'s shiny brown shoes and moved his eyes up to his blue coll**ar**.

“You're dis**missed**,” he said and then took an**oth**er step and st**ood** in front of Neal Pr**ice**. Neal and I have been in the same class**es** since the second gr**ade** and we're the same age, but he was tw**ice** my size. E**ven** his head was two times big**ger** than mine. Reese didn't e**ven** bother ask**ing** his name; he waved his hand then Neal **turn**ed and **walk**ed a**way** grinn**ing**. The prin**ci**pal took an**oth**er step and now he was stand**ing** in front of me.

He st**ood** so close that I could see the gray hairs in**side** his nose move up and down ev**ery** time he breathed. It was gross. I **look**ed a**way** at the crowd and saw my br**others**. They **look**ed the way that I felt, scared. “Young man, face for**ward**!” Reese **yell**ed. I didn't want Dan and Rob to tease me when we got home so I st**ood** the same way Dan did that time at the zoo; I didn't move a muscle.

“Is this yours?” Prin**ci**pal Reese **ask**ed point**ing** the hat at me.

“I think so,” I **whisper**ed.

He **lean**ed in to**ward** me and **ask**ed, “*NP* huh?” He paused and squint**ed** his eyes. “What's your name?”

“Nick P**ear**son.”

“P**ear**son?” he asked, t**a**king a step back. “You're a P**ear**son?” I **look**ed at the crowd. Ev**eryone** **look**ed as nervous as I felt.

◊ ◊ ◊

I heard about Prin**ci**pal Reese a few years ago and he was mean. He **yell**ed at kids, gave out de**ten**tions for no reason, and canceled re**cess** whene**v**er he felt like it. My br**other**, Dan, said that Reese wasn't al**ways** that way. He said that Prin**ci**pal Reese used to be fun. He **dress**ed up as the school mas**cot** at bas**ket**ball games and threw out gold-**cover**ed choc**o**lates to the crowd dur**ing** half**time**. Dan said that Reese e**ven** hired a real D.J. for a few of the dances instead of lett**ing** Mr. Rivers, the shop teach**er**, play with his heavy met**al** band. One time af**ter** a big state test, Prin**ci**pal Reese bought pizza for the en**tire** school as a re**ward** for do**ing** so well. He was probably the cool**est** prin**ci**pal ev**er** un**til** my br**other** Rob came a**long**.

Dan was a trou**ble**ma**ker** in six**th** gr**ade** and all the teach**ers** knew it. They didn't like it but they could handle it. He made noises dur**ing** class, wrote on the desks and **talk**ed back to teach**er**s; but when Rob came to Wood**son** Middle School it was like they com**pe**ted to see who could cause the most trouble. If Dan **skipp**ed a class, so did Rob. If Rob de**fla**ted a bas**ket**ball dur**ing** gym class Dan de**fla**ted all the bas**ket**balls. If Dan threw food at Rob, Rob threw food at ev**eryone** in the caf**e**ter**i**a. That's how the food fight start**ed** and end**ed** up on Mr. Gr**een**'s car.

Prin**ci**pal Reese want**ed** to prove a point to show them and all the other kids at Wood**son** Middle School that he wouldn't ac**cept** bad behavior any**more** from any**one**. He **bann**ed Dan and Rob from the Hall**o**ween dance. They felt badly for a while; not about mess**ing** up Mr. Gr**een**'s car but about miss**ing** the dance.

They pout**ed** around the house and for a couple of days at school they were off **everyone**'s r**a**dar. Prin**ci**pal Reese start**ed** to soft**en** up, too. He was st**ill** a nice guy so he end**ed** their pun**ish**ment early. That was a big mis**take**. See, my br**others** knew that Reese would call off their pun**ish**ment if they **seem**ed sorry enough, and they were right.

Two hours be**fore** the dance start**ed**, my br**others** **walk**ed to school and **sneak**ed in af**ter** the D.J. set up. Tables with food and drinks were dec**orated** with orange and black con**fet**ti, and tiny carved pump**kins** were **fill**ed with candy. Once Dan and Rob were alone, they **pour**ed bottle af**ter** bottle of cook**ing** oil from the caf**e**ter**i**a all over the gym floor. Ev**ery** inch of the gym was slippery ex**cept** a small path from the door to the D.J.'s booth. Dan said it took them e**lev**en minutes to turn the school gym in**to** an ice rink. They **even** greased the walls!

The D.J. **play**ed music in**side** while the line out**side** grew. Prin**ci**pal Reese and five other teach**ers** were there to make sure the kids behaved. Ev**eryone**, **even** the prin**ci**pal, was **dress**ed in costume; ev**eryone** ex**cept** Dan and Rob. They st**ood** at the back of the line in the clothes they wore to school earlier that day. Prin**ci**pal Reese smiled and **open**ed the doors then **stepp**ed a**side** to let the kids run to the dance floor. None of them took more than five steps be**fore** they fell. Some kids tried to grab the walls to stand but fell hard**er.**

When Prin**ci**pal Reese heard the com**mo**tion, he ran in. He slid half**way** across the floor in**to** one of the tables with food. He hit hard. All of the food that was on the table land**ed** on top of him. Sand**wich**es, cookies, chips, salsa, and cup**cakes** with icing all piled on Prin**ci**pal Reese. He tried to stand and this time fell in**to** the table with the drinks. Juice in tiny red cups flew in the air and land**ed** on him. He was de**ter**mined to stand up but when**ev**er he tried, some**one** else sli**ding** across the floor **knock**ed him back down. It was use**less**. He sat up on his knees to see what **happen**ed. Hun**dreds** of kids were crawl**ing**, roll**ing**, and spinn**ing** on the slippery floor. No one was stand**ing** ex**cept** Dan and Rob. Prin**ci**pal Reese hasn't been the same since.

He sus**pend**ed my br**others** for a whole week. When they got back to school, Prin**ci**pal Reese had an**oth**er meet**ing** with my mom and dad and told them if Dan and Rob caused any more trouble he would kick them out of school. My parents took that seriously and Dan and Rob got bet**ter** at not be**ing** caught.

Now Prin**ci**pal Reese was stand**ing** in front of me look**ing** mean as ev**er**. He c**leared** his throat, bent down, and **lean**ed in clo**ser**. He **whisper**ed a**gain**, "You're a P**ear**son?" His face was so close that his nose al**most touch**ed mine. I fr**oze**. I want**ed** to say *yes, but it's not what you think,* but my mouth was dry. All I could do was nod my head. He straightened up, **look**ed me in the eyes, and then smiled.

Reese **walk**ed a**way** and be**fore** I knew it, I was stand**ing** alone in front of the whole school. I want**ed** to run and hide, but I couldn't move. Dan **push**ed his way through the crowd to**ward** me and Rob **follow**ed.

"Nicky, that was awe**some**!" Dan said as he put his arm on my shoulder.

"Yeah, you're really a P**ear**son now!" Rob add**ed**.

"What do you mean?"

Dan said, "Don't you un**der**stand what just **happen**ed? He smiled at you!" I shrugged my shoulders.

He said, "Reese nev**er** smiles."

"So."

"So? So now you're the man."

Chapter Six

Recess was over and we didn't even get to play flag football. Chris and I walked back into the building and out of nowhere I heard "Hey Nick," and "Pearson, what's up!" from boys and girls I didn't know.

"You're the man! Everyone knows your name now," Chris said. He was right! Everyone did know my name and it felt good. It was only the first day of school and because Reese smiled at me, people liked me. Chris stopped walking and said, "Hey, you never told me how your notebook ended up with Principal Reese."

"Huh?" I stopped walking and pretended I didn't know what he meant.

"You know . . . Principal Reese found your notebook in the science lab."

"Oh, yeah, well . . . I left it in the science lab after class." I took off walking again.

"I know that, but you ran back to get it. How'd you forget it again?"

I was hoping that he wouldn't ask that. I let out a deep breath and said, "I accidentally opened the cages and dropped my notebook on the floor. That's where Principal Reese found it."

"How'd you *accidentally* open the cages?" he asked in between laughing.

I stopped walking again and blurted out, "I forgot my notebook in the science lab and I found it on the teacher's desk and that crazy ferret scared me and I fell back and hit the switch." Chris burst out laughing. He probably thought I was lame for being so lame.

◊ ◊ ◊

Back in the build**ing**, I **grabb**ed my back**pack** from my lock**er** and **walk**ed up**stairs** to my next class. Be**fore** to**day**, I had only been to the prin**ci**pal's off**ice** so the second floor was br**and** new to me and I was lost. Nor**mal**ly, I would walk around on my own look**ing** for the room but to**day** I wasn't scared to ask for help. Kids didn't seem too cool to talk to me an**y**more. I **stopp**ed a boy in the hall and said, "Hey, where's the com**pu**ter lab?"

"Come on! I'll show you," he said. I **follow**ed him half**way** down the hall un**til** he point**ed** to the room.

"Thanks."

"No prob**lem**, Nick," he said. He knew my name! It was ex**act**ly what I want**ed** — no more Nate!

I wasn't nervous any**more** about walk**ing** in**to** a new class**room**, not e**ven** a little bit. This time, I **open**ed the door and **walk**ed in smil**ing**. The teacher didn't no**tice** me but all the kids in the first row **look**ed up and a couple of them smiled back. Be**tween** each com**pu**ter on ev**er**y row was a red and white sign that had "NO FOOD OR DRINK" written on it with a picture of a stick of gum in the middle of a red circle with a line drawn through it. On the board, scribbled in white chalk was "No candy. No talk**ing**. No sharing com**pu**ters. No horse**play** around the com**pu**ters. No surf**ing** the web with**out** per**mission**." She had a lot of rules.

I **walk**ed to the back of the room and sat in an empty ch**air** next to the wall. More kids **walk**ed in and sat down, too. I rec**og**nized one of the girls who **walk**ed in from my el**e**men**tar**y school, but I didn't know her name. She **look**ed around the room then **walk**ed by five empty seats and sat next to me. I didn't move — or blink my eyes, or breathe. I didn't know her last year, but I knew she was pop**u**lar. The teacher **walk**ed to the front of the room and **clapp**ed her hands three times. Af**ter** ev**eryone** got qui**et**, she **look**ed up and down the aisle at us kids. She didn't smile or tell us her name or e**ven** stand there very long. She **turn**ed around and **walk**ed to her desk and start**ed** talk**ing** about com**pu**ters be**ing** im**por**tant to our future and that we should know how to use them. She said we'd learn how to make our own web pages and by the end of the school year we'd all be good at ty**ping**.

Her name was Mrs. Arn**old** and she **talk**ed about the class**room** rules, **talk**ed about u**sing** the in**ter**net, and **talk**ed about not talk**ing** while *she* was talk**ing**. The bell didn't e**ven** ring yet, but she went on and on un**til** it did, then some**one** **knock**ed on the door. "May I speak with you for a mo**ment**?" a man asked. I couldn't see him, but I knew the voice. I **lean**ed for**ward** to get a look at his face and ac**ci**dent**al**ly **bump**ed the girl's arm next to me.

"Sorry."

She smiled and said, "It's okay."

I **lean**ed back in my ch**air** but st**ill** tried to listen to what they were say**ing**. I couldn't hear them, but I knew it was about me. I caught Mrs. Arn**old** sneak a peek at me then the man **stepp**ed in**to** the room and **look**ed at me, too. It was Prin**ci**pal Reese.

"You're Nick, right?" The girl next to me **ask**ed. I nod**ded** my head. *How does she know my name?* I wasn't sure but I didn't care now. I want**ed** to know what Reese and Mrs. Arn**old** had to say about me. Did he come all the way up here just for this?

"My name is Kelly," she said. I smiled and nod**ded** my head in her di**rec**tion, but my eyes were on the door un**til** Reese **walk**ed a**way**. When I **look**ed back to Kelly, she was still smi**ling**. Girls nev**er** talk to me un**less** they have to or if it's for a class as**sign**ment. I told her that I re**mem**ber her from last year. She smiled but I could tell she didn't re**mem**ber me.

When Mrs. Arn**old** **walk**ed back to her desk she **watch**ed me like a hawk. Ev**eryone** had been act**ing** strange all day. First, Mr. Gr**een** was a jerk to me, and Prin**ci**pal Reese smiled for the first time in a year, at me. Then, kids I'd nev**er** met be**fore** spoke to me dur**ing** lun**ch** and now Mrs. Arn**old** stared at me as if I'd done some**thing** wrong. May**be** Reese told her about my hat that he found. Or may**be** he figured out that the yel**low** note**book** was mine. What**ev**er it was, it wasn't good.

"Turn on your com**pu**ters," Mrs. Arn**old** said as she **walk**ed to the first row of kids.

She told us that these com**pu**ters cost a lot of money and that if we were caught play**ing** around with them we wouldn't be able to use them.

She **walk**ed down all four aisles but when she got to my row, she **stopp**ed, **turn**ed around, and **walk**ed back to her desk.

"Type your name and a short par**a**graph about your**self**. Double-space it. Use spell check. And when you're done, be sure to save the doc**u**ment," Mrs. Arn**old** shout**ed** across the room.

I wasn't worried be**cause** I knew how to do all of those things — my br**other** Rob taught me. I moved the mouse around but no**thing happen**ed. A few minutes **pass**ed and ev**eryone** was click**ing** a**way** on their key**boards** ex**cept** me. Kelly **lean**ed over and **ask**ed, "You need some help?"

She **reach**ed over be**fore** I could answer and **press**ed the but**ton** on the com**pu**ter screen at the ex**act** same time that Mrs. Arn**old look**ed up.

"There should be only one stu**dent** on each com**pu**ter," Mrs. Arn**old yell**ed at me e**ven** though Kelly was the one lean**ing** over to my com**pu**ter.

I raised my hand to ask Mrs. Arn**old** for help, but she ig**nored** me for so long that my arm be**gan** to feel heavy. I had to use my right hand to hold up my left arm but that didn't work either.

"What but**tons** did you press?" I **whisper**ed to Kelly. "Mine isn't work**ing**." She **turn**ed to answer when the teacher ran from her desk to our row. Now Mrs. Arn**old** was stand**ing** right be**hind** me.

"Niiick Pearrrson," she sang my name. I **look**ed over my shoulder and smelled her per**fume**. It re**mind**ed me of my grand**mother**'s base**ment** **after** it rains. "I know your br**others** and I heard about you. You will not cause trouble in my class**room**. Do you un**der**stand?" she said loud enough for the kids around me to hear. The whole class probably heard. I **turn**ed back to face my com**pu**ter and nod**ded** my head.

Mrs. Arn**old** **walk**ed a**way** as fast as she **walk**ed over. Kelly typed on her key**board**, pretend**ing** she didn't hear any**thing**. I was scared to move any**thing** other than my fing**ers** so I **press**ed more but**tons** but st**ill** no**thing** **happen**ed. If I didn't do the as**sign**ment, Mrs. Arn**old** would think that she was right about me. And I knew that she wasn't.

When the teach**er** wasn't look**ing**, I slid out of my ch**air** and bent down un**der** the table. Look**ing** around on the floor, I could see a bun**ch** of cords so I pulled on them un**til** one was in my hand. *It's un**plugged**!* The surge pro**tec**tor was full so I **lean**ed over to the wall out**let** and **plugg**ed in the cord. The com**pu**ter made a buzz**ing** sound when it **turn**ed on. I want**ed** to say to Mrs. Arn**old**, '*See, I'm not a trouble maker! I'm just try**ing** to do my work!*' But as soon as I sat back in my ch**air** ev**erything** went dark — not just in our room but the hall**way**, too. It was a black**out**! Ev**eryone** went nuts. Kelly **scream**ed. People start**ed** to bang on the desks or slide their ch**airs** across the floor. One of the boys in front of me made fart**ing** sounds; ev**eryone** burst out laugh**ing**. This would have been funny if it wasn't my fault.

"Settle down, children!" Mrs. Arn**old** shout**ed** and **clapp**ed over the noise. "We must sit qui**et**ly and wait for in**struc**tions."

A couple of seconds l**a**ter, an**oth**er teach**er** came in**to** our room and told us that the e**mer**gen**cy** lights would come on soon and when they do, to walk down to the gym where the back**up** lights were on. Once the blue e**mer**gen**cy** lights came on in the class**room** and the hall**way**, Mrs. Arn**old** told us to grab our back**packs**. We lined up at the door and she led us down to the gym.

Our class **walk**ed in**to** the dark hall**way**. **Even** with the e**mer**gen**cy** lights on, the only thing I could see was the floor. I **walk**ed with my hand a**gain**st the wall and **follow**ed the shoes of the kid in front of me. Stu**dents** and teach**ers** came from ev**ery** di**rec**tion try**ing** to get to the stairs. Some kids **push**ed and shoved so I **stepp**ed out of line a**gain**st the wall and wait**ed** for them to pass. The hall**way** was crowd**ed** and noisy but over the adults yell**ing** at kids, and kids laugh**ing** and scream**ing** I heard my name. I ran back in line to listen.

"I heard he **open**ed the cages and let out the science an**i**mals."

"Really!? I heard that he flood**ed** the bath**room**."

"No way! Nick is so cool!"

I couldn't believe it. *How do they know about the science an**i**mals? And why do they think that I flood**ed** the bath**room** on purpose?* I **walk**ed with the rest of my class down the stairs to the gym where Chris found me. He had heard, too.

"Hey, why are people say**ing** that you flood**ed** the bath**room**?"

"I don't know, but it's not all bad. Some**one** said that I was cool!" Chris **look**ed at me as if I had two heads.

"You won't be so cool when you tell Prin**ci**pal Reese what really **happen**ed," he said and then **laugh**ed.

Af**ter** a long pause he said, "You are go**ing** to tell him what **happen**ed, right?" I ig**nored** him and kept walk**ing**. Honestly, I was just fine lett**ing** ev**eryone** think that I was cool. Chris didn't like it. He said, "Look, I just don't want you to get in trouble over some stu**pid** ac**ci**dents. If you tell Prin**ci**pal Reese the truth he'll probably go easy on you." He was right. They were just a bun**ch** of silly ac**ci**dents. Prin**ci**pal Reese would un**der**stand. Or would he think that I was just like my br**others**? I didn't know if tell**ing** the truth was worth losing my new friends. This was the first time that people went out of their way to be nice to me; the first time that a girl want**ed** to sit by me.

What if I told about the ac**ci**dents and Reese didn't believe me. He would call my parents to the school for a meet**ing** and they would be mad — no, mad**der** than mad. I was the only kid left in my house who didn't cause any trouble. They'd have a hun**dred** questions when we got home. And what about school? My new friends would think I was a dork for be**ing** clumsy and then tell**ing** on my**self**. I didn't e**ven** want to think about what my br**others** would say. But if I kept my mouth shut, ev**eryone** would st**ill** think that I was cool and Prin**ci**pal Reese couldn't pun**ish** me.

◊ ◊ ◊

It was a mad**house** in the gym. Ev**er**y kid in school was sitt**ing** in the bleach**ers**; some were shout**ing**; some were stomp**ing** in the stands, and some were throw**ing** spit**balls** around. Noise came from ev**er**y di**rec**tion. Chris and I were probably the only kids who weren't talk**ing**. I want**ed** to tell him all the cool things that **happen**ed to**day:** Mrs. Go**mez** be**ing** nice; how it felt to have so many kids talk to me; and about the girl in com**pu**ter class want**ing** to sit next to me. But he wouldn't un**der**stand.

Mr. Free**man**, the gym teacher, blew the whistle that was around his neck but it only add**ed** to the noise be**cause** most kids didn't e**ven** no**tice** it. He held a bull**horn** with his left hand and with the other he lif**ted** the sil**ver** whistle by its strings and **press**ed it to his mouth a**gain**. He took a deep breath, but Prin**ci**pal Reese **walk**ed through the gym doors be**fore** he let it out. The clo**ser** Reese got to the middle of the floor, the quiet**er** the room be**came**. He did a bet**ter** job at shutt**ing** ev**erybod**y up than that whistle.

One of the gym doors **open**ed and a couple of kids **walk**ed in late. Reese gave them the look — you know the kind grownups give to kids that means 'this is the first and last warn**ing**' — and he meant business. Those boys ran to the bleach**ers** and sat down be**fore** the door e**ven** closed. The only noise now was Mrs. Arn**old**'s shoes click**ing** across the floor as she **walk**ed to the circle of teach**ers** in the middle of the gym. Mr. Free**man** **pass**ed the bull**horn** to Reese, but Reese **push**ed it a**way**.

I guess he liked to yell.

“One of you thought it would be funny to cause a black**out**,” Reese said and point**ed** his long, fat fing**er** around the gym. He said, “When I find out who you are, and I will find out, I guarantee you won’t be laugh**ing**.” The prin**ci**pal **stepp**ed over to the teach**er**’s huddle, said a few words to them then pulled a**way**. He st**ood** alone look**ing** over the crowd. Mr. Gr**een** and Mrs. Arn**old** be**gan** talk**ing** to each other and then Mr. Gr**een** **look**ed up and found me in the bleach**ers**.

Reese start**ed** walk**ing** a**gain**. He said, “I believe that the same stu**dent** **open**ed the cages in the science lab. That stu**dent** is a six**th** gr**a**der.” He **stopp**ed walk**ing** and said, “All I have to do now is wait.” *Wait? What the heck was he wait**ing** for!?* Kids be**gan** moving around in their seats and start**ed** to whis**per**. Prin**ci**pal Reese raised his hand and the gym was qui**et** a**gain**. He walked toward the gym doors but **stopp**ed and said, “Oh, and if any of you know what **happen**ed and you don’t re**port** it to the adults here,” he said point**ing** to the teach**ers** in the middle of the floor, “you, too, will be **punish**ed.”

Chris sat like a statue un**til** now. He hit my arm with his el**bow** and shook his head. I **look**ed at him and **wonder**ed if he was worried about me gett**ing** in trouble for *do**ing*** all those things or him**self** for *know**ing***? But I guess I al**ready** knew.

Two sum**mers** ago, my neighbor's bike was sto**len** from his garage and I saw the whole thing. Actually, I only saw David rid**ing** a**way** on the bike, but I knew he stole it. He stole every**thing**: soccer balls; toys left in the yard; one time, he e**ven** stole a dog. That day, I **walk**ed home from Chris' house and saw David fly**ing** by on that red and black beach cruiser. I knew it was Mr. Good**man**'s bike be**cause** he brought it over to our house earlier that day to use my dad's air pump.

The next day, on our way home from the park, Mr. Good**man** **stopp**ed Chris and me and **ask**ed us if we had seen or heard an**y**thing. We both said no. Ten minutes af**ter** we got to my house, David **knock**ed on the front door. He want**ed** to make sure that I kept my mouth shut about what I saw. I told him I did. Chris over**heard** ev**erything**. He told me it was wrong to keep qui**et** about the sto**len** bike and that if I didn't tell Mr. Good**man** what I knew, he would. I **begg**ed Chris not to say an**y**thing be**cause** if David e**ven** *thought* that I rat**ted** on him he would come look**ing** for me. I was scared and didn't know what to do so I didn't do an**y**thing.

The next day, Chris told Mr. Good**man** about the sto**len** bike, sort of. He didn't tell him that I was there be**cause** he didn't want it to get back to David. The prob**lem** was that Mr. Good**man** thought Chris' story sound**ed** fishy. He couldn't un**der**stand how Chris knew who had ta**ken** the bike if he wasn't there, so he drove Chris home and told his parents what *he* thought **happen**ed. Chris had no way of proving how he knew David had ta**ken** the bike with**out** tell**ing** on me. He was ground**ed** for a month and he didn't talk to me for an**oth**er two weeks.

When I finally saw him six weeks later, he said that if I had told Mr. Goodman the truth, he wouldn't have been grounded for half the summer.

◊ ◊ ◊

He was right. And sitting in the crowded gym now, I knew that Chris was right again. I felt hot all over. I wondered if smoke was blowing from my ears like in those cartoons. The sweat rolling down my back made my shirt stick to my skin. I had to tell Reese that I caused the blackout, let out those animals, *and* accidentally flooded the bathroom. If I didn't, someone else would. I didn't know how so many kids knew about the science animals, or why they thought I let them out on purpose. *How many of them would still want to be my friends if they knew that it was just an accident?* I wiped my forehead but my hands were sweaty, too. I looked around the gym and no one else seemed to feel the heat — not the way I did. I peeked over at Chris. He was looking down at his feet. I felt badly and wanted to speak up and tell the truth but my mouth was so dry. I took two big gulps then cleared my throat.

Everyone watched me . . . and I mean *everyone*. Kids sitting at the bottom of the bleachers turned their necks trying to look at me. The teachers standing in the middle of the floor took turns watching me. I even felt the kids sitting behind me looking. Nobody said anything, but they didn't have to — the way the adults treated me and those kids in the hall talked about me — I knew what they were thinking.

But I want**ed** Prin**ci**pal Reese and the teach**ers** to see that I wasn't just an**oth**er [illegible]son. I didn't care any**more** if kids liked me. I want**ed** to sh**out** so that ev**ery**one in the gym could hear me, but I didn't know what to say. The thoughts in my head **bump**ed around a**gain**st each other. Finally, the words moved like a snail up through my throat. I wiped the sweat from my hands on to my jeans then st**ood** up and Prin**ci**pal Reese **look**ed right at me! No, *through* me! May**be** he could see in**side** my head and read my mind. He **look**ed as if he want**ed** to yell a**gain**. And this time he would have a good reason.

Be**fore** I could o**pen** my mouth Reese said, "Al**right** children, you are dis**missed**." Now ev**erybod**y was stand**ing** up and Prin**ci**pal Reese **walk**ed a**way** to**ward** the doors. *Whew!* I **turn**ed to see what Reese was look**ing** at; it was the clock right above my head. When he got to the doors he **stopp**ed, **turn**ed, and said, "I'll be watch**ing** you." He point**ed** to me then he said, "And you. And you. And you." He point**ed** around the gym. Ev**eryone** ran down the bleach**ers** and out the double doors.

Chapter Seven

I stood in the doorway until enough people passed by for me to blend in then I ducked behind a couple of kids and followed them outside. I didn't want Chris or any teachers to see me. All of this ducking and hiding made me hot again. I began to sweat and my heart felt like it would beat out of my chest. I could almost hear it pounding over the buses' engines. Cars drove up and parked at the curb waiting to pick up kids. I wish I had a ride to take me home. But I didn't. *Should I run or wait around to look for my brothers so that I wouldn't have to walk alone?* I hid behind one tall kid then ran to hide behind another. Then I dropped behind a trash can. Kids walked around and acted so normal.

From behind the trashcan, I looked up and down the sidewalk, left then right, then left again. The entire Woodson Middle School was outside in the schoolyard. But Rob and Dan were nowhere in sight. I looked straight ahead and focused on a row of bushes at the end of the yard. I knew once I passed by that, I'd be off school property and out of sight from the other kids; but first I had to get there. I stood up from behind that smelly trashcan and took a step, then another, then another. By the tenth or eleventh step my feet were slamming against the sidewalk — I was marching.

No matter where I looked, I saw someone new looking at me. I had become *that* kid. You know the one no one wants to talk to, but everyone talks about. Yep, that's me. But I can't worry about that now. The only thing that matters is getting home.

I didn't e**ven** care that I had to walk home by my**self**, or that my best friend in the whole world is mad at me.

I took wide steps and got half**way** across the yard in no time. A group of kids was stand**ing** on the side**walk** and they were in my way. I could say no**thing** and hope that they would move or I could yell '*Get out of my way!'* I was a couple steps a**way** when those kids broke up their circle; I **walk**ed right through the middle and didn't e**ven** say thank you. I just **walk**ed.

The bus**es** were here but the yard was st**ill** full of kids jump**ing** rope, hugg**ing**, and play**ing** catch. Some were e**ven** sitt**ing** un**der** the trees in the shade do**ing** their home**work**. I think I was the only one go**ing** home. An**oth**er group of kids st**ood** in my way now; it was Denise Parks and four of her friends. At first, I wasn't sure if they saw me but then Denise be**gan** to stare at me. She **lean**ed over and **whisper**ed to the girl next to her. Then that girl said some**thing** to the girl next to her, and the one next to her un**til** all five of them were look**ing** at me. When I got clo**ser**, I thought one of them might say some**thing** to me but instead they split apart, one by one, just like the first group. That was cool. I didn't e**ven** have to say any**thing**; they just moved. I want**ed** to laugh but then I saw Chris. He **toss**ed a foot**ball** back and forth to Mark. I **look**ed far**ther** down the side**walk** at those bush**es**. I could walk right by Chris and pre**tend** that I didn't see him or may**be** hide be**tween** the school bus**es** un**til** he left.

I **stepp**ed to**ward** the curb and was al**most** out of sight from the rest of the kids when I heard some**one** call my name. I pretend**ed** I didn't hear it and kept walk**ing** then I heard it a**gain**. "Wait up Nick!" Kelly **yell**ed, rush**ing** to**ward** me. I didn't know what she want**ed**, but I was glad it was her call**ing** me and not some**one** else. I st**ood** st**ill** and wait**ed** for her to say some**thing**, but she didn't.

"Uhhh, hey Kelly, what's up?"

"No**thing** much . . . just want**ed** to say good**bye**."

*This girl ran across the school**yard** just to say 'good**bye**'?!*

"Uhhh, okay. Bye."

She smiled and then **walk**ed a**way**. Now I could see Chris and Mark head**ing** my way, but they st**ill** didn't see me. I had time to run or hide, or both. I **look**ed around for a good place to go but the bus**es** be**gan** to drive off. I had to run. My brain **yell**ed, "GO!" but my feet didn't get the mess**age** in time. It was too late. They saw me. Chris waved, said some**thing** to Mark, then Mark smiled. *What did Chris say? And why was Mark smil**ing**?*

"Hey, where have you been?" Chris **ask**ed.

My brain went back to hi**ding** be**hind** those tall kids, then that garbage can. *What was I supposed to say? I've been dodg**ing** you.* I said, "I . . . I've been around."

"Do**ing** what?" Chris asked.

I shrugged my shoulders. I didn't know how to answer that. Chris and Mark **stood** at the curb and **watch**ed me walk a**way**.

“He’s so cool,” Mark said un**der** his breath. I **stopp**ed, **turn**ed around, and **walk**ed back to where they were stand**ing**.

I asked, “What did you say?”

“I said you’re cool, man, for do**ing** all those crazy things,” Mark said.

I **look**ed over at Chris. He was smi**ling** and nodd**ing** his head. Earlier, he wouldn’t **even** look at me. Now he was grinn**ing** from ear to ear. I **wonder**ed what changed his mind. And to**mor**row I **plann**ed to find out.

When I **turn**ed the first corn**er**, I felt a little bet**ter**. I could see my block from here. I was glad to see my house. I want**ed** to walk through the front door and for**get** that this day **happen**ed but I knew that was impossible. Dad would ask about my class**es** and Mom would want to know if I made any new friends. Actually, those questions would be easier to answer than the ones Dan and Rob would ask. My head hurt.

My br**others** would clown me the way they al**ways** do. Rob would st**art** by say**ing**, “Nicky, I heard that Reese smiled at you be**cause** you’re best friends.” Then Dan would say, “I heard you **open**ed those cages be**cause** you thought there were **stuff**ed animals in**side**.” Af**ter**ward they would laugh at me and tell our parents every**thing**.

I took a deep breath and held it as I un**locked** the front door. When I **push**ed it o**pen**, I heard voices coming from the living room but no one was there. It was just the TV. Last month, Dan **stay**ed out past his cur**few** and had to sneak back in the house. He was caught. But the next day, he taught Rob and me which steps squeak and which ones don’t. My shoes barely **touch**ed the wood as I **climb**ed the stairs to my room.

Then I heard my dad say, "I don't believe this!" I knew this would hap**pen**. Rob loved to get Dan and me in trouble. He probably ran home and told our parents what I did. "What are you *think**ing***!?" Dad **yell**ed. I **stopp**ed half**way** up the stairs. All af**ter**noon I've been think**ing** about how I would ex**plain** my day, now I was too tired to try. When I **turn**ed around my dad was walk**ing** in**to** the living room, talk**ing** to the tel**e**vision screen, watch**ing** a base**ball** game. He didn't e**ven** know that I was home. I **pick**ed up the pace and ran to the top of the stairs, straight to my room. And when I got there Rob and Dan were sit**ting** on my bed.

I st**ood** in the door**way** want**ing** to scream *"Get out of my room!!!"* But that would've given my br**others** an**oth**er reason to stay and tease me. Be**sides**, Mom would be home from work soon and she might hear and would want to know what was go**ing** on. I pretend**ed** they didn't bother me. Their eyes **follow**ed me across the room to my desk. This was the craziest day of my life but it felt kind of cool to have Dan and Rob's at**ten**tion. For once, they treat**ed** me like one of them and not just their little br**other**.

"Nicky, what took you so long to get home from school?" Dan asked. His voice sound**ed** strange. He was worried.

"I had some**thing** to do."

"Some**thing** like what?" Rob **ask**ed then **look**ed at Dan. I wasn't sure how to answer but any**thing** I said now would make them ask more questions. I shrugged my shoulders then took off my back**pack** and sat down at my desk.

Even though I couldn't see them, I knew my brothers were watching me.

If I stalled for another five minutes, I'll bet they would just watch and wait. My cheeks puffed up and a smile broke out on my face, but I didn't want them to see. I turned my backpack upside down and dumped everything on the desk then I moved around the books and papers trying to look busy. My back was still turned toward them, but I knew they were making faces at each other wondering what I was up to. And I loved it!

I turned to face them and said, "I was taking care of stuff." Dan said that same thing to me when I asked him why he missed curfew. It made me mad that he and Rob would never tell me anything but now I understood why. It was more fun keeping them guessing. My brothers got the hint that I wasn't going to say much and they left.

I waited until I heard the sound of their footsteps fade away then I walked across the room. I flopped down on my bed and for the first time all day I felt relaxed. The light over my bed was so bright it was too much, so I closed my eyes. This entire day was too much so I pretended that it never happened. *What if I would have walked into Mr. Green's class and he didn't recognize me? He would not have been a jerk to me or used Lucy to scare me in front of the entire class. What if I never left my notebook and didn't have to go back and get it . . . I would have never opened those cages. Principal Reese would have had no reason to come into my English class and yell at Mr. Matthews. Yeah . . . that would have been a good day.*

But no! I want**ed** to make friends and look where it got me: alone in my room on the first day of school. Chris and his new best friend Mark were probably out**side** some**where** right now play**ing** catch.

*What**ev**er!* I can't worry about that now. My mom and dad would be up here any minute ask**ing** about my day. I had to think fast. I'll bet one of my br**others** ran to the living room and told our dad that I was act**ing** weird. But may**be** not. If he had heard that, he would have flown up here by now ask**ing** a ton of questions. I lied in bed so long that the sun was be**gin**ning to set. And the room was gett**ing** dark. I got up once to turn off the light.

My room got dark**er** and dark**er** and I felt like I was fa**ding** a**way**. I could hide here for**ev**er. But that was silly. Soon**er** or l**a**ter my dad's base**ball** game would go off or my mom would come look**ing** for me. I thought how yes**ter**day I was just Nick, Dan and Rob's little br**other**. But to**day** I was the badd**est** kid in six**th** gr**ade**.

Made in the USA
Columbia, SC
05 August 2018